Shortly before going to print, the cat who this story is based upon passed away. This is dedicated in honor of CougaMongaMingaMan and to each of my beloved companion animals. Also, to all of the unloved, unwanted animals throughout the world.

- Nancy Scalabroni

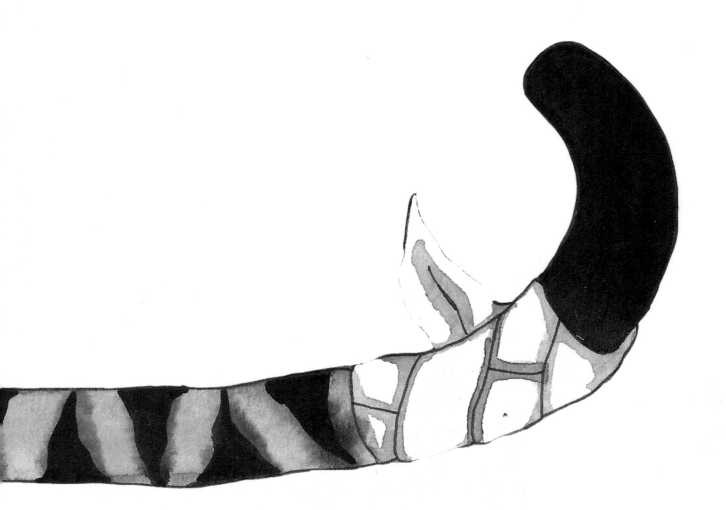

www.mascotbooks.com

CougaMongaMingaMan

For more information, please contact:

Mascot Books
560 Herndon Parkway #120
Herndon, VA 20170
info@mascotbooks.com

Library of Congress Control Number: 2013950820

CPSIA Code: PRT1113A
ISBN-10: 1620864991
ISBN-13: 9781620864999

Printed in the United States

CougaMongaMingaMan

The cat with the very long name. . .and the very long tail

Nancy Scalabroni
illustrated by Terri Kelleher

CougaMongaMingaMan had the longest name of any cat in the neighborhood. In addition to having the longest name, he also had the longest tail. The humans he lived with would say to him, "Cougie, you sure are a character."

CougaMongaMingaMan would look at them and think, *And you sure are privileged to enjoy my company.*

Each day he and his friends, the other neighborhood cats, would gather in the vacant lot at the end of the street to share their news. Sometimes they would talk about how odd humans are and at other times, they discussed their own kind.

Today the topic was about a new family that had moved in, which prompted a conversation about names.

Tonto the Tabby said, "I saw a new cat when her humans were moving in and I asked her name but she ran and hid."

"Silly," said Miss Pittypat, a lovely Maine Coon. "All of this is new to her and she's probably afraid."

"I live next door to her," said Snow, a pure white beauty. "Let a girl handle this."

"By the way," Snow continued, "how in the world did your humans come up with the name CougaMongaMingaMan? Not that I don't like it."

All eyes turned to CougaMongaMingaMan. "Well," he explained, "it started with the name Cougar because that's what I remind them of." Tonto and Miss Pittypat nodded in agreement. He continued, "Then Cougar turned into Couga, sometimes CougaMonga, and they just kept adding. Most of the time they call me Cougie or CougarMan."

"Sounds like they have trouble making up their minds," said Tonto.

"Well, it's more original than what my humans came up with," said Snow.

"I only hope they stop while they can still say it,"
said CougaMongaMingaMan, and everyone laughed.

A tinkling bell sounded nearby and Miss Pittypat got up and stretched. "My humans are calling me to dinner. See you tomorrow."

"Bye," they called back.

The next day, Snow informed the group about her encounter with the new girl in town.

"Her name is Two-Face and she's very shy, although she said she would love to join us. She said her humans don't let her out every day and today she has to have a bath."

Tonto felt the hair on his neck stand on end. "No way," he declared. "My human's might get a surprise on the carpet if they tried that on me."

Miss Pittypat looked at Tonto and flicked her tail in the air several times before tucking it around her feet. "You're so naughty," she said.

All of this talk about baths made CougaMongaMingaMan uneasy and he changed the subject.

"This is the tallest the grass has ever grown in this lot. It's been a great place to go unnoticed."

"Oh, we notice you, Cougar," said Miss Pittypat.
"Your tail is so long, I saw you coming from a block away!"

CougaMongaMingaMan's eyes widened when Snow and Tonto confirmed that his tail looked like a flagpole as he walked with it sticking straight up in the air.

"Well, it's not the first time I've been accused of having a monkey's tail," he responded.

"Better that than a monkey's face," said Miss Pittypat and they all howled.

"On that note, I think I'll take my leave and go beg for some tuna treats," said CougaMongaMingaMan as he turned to leave the group.

"Bye," said everyone.
"See you tomorrow."

"Bye," responded CougaMongaMingaMan, and he purposely raised his tail to its full height as he walked back home.

It was muggy and humid the next time the group gathered.
Tonto, Miss Pittypat, and Snow were all discussing how hot it
had been during the day and how lazy they had felt.

"I saw a lizard right in front of my nose and
couldn't have cared less," said Tonto.

"I was so hot I didn't move an inch when my humans
rang the bell to eat," stated Miss Pittypat.

"I went inside and stayed in front of a fan," said Snow.

The one thing they all noticed was the absence of CougaMongaMingaMan.

"He never misses a meeting," said Snow. "Do you think he might be upset because we teased him about his tail?"

"No, no! He's probably being smart and staying inside where it's cool," said Tonto.

Miss Pittypat agreed, "He's not sensitive. He knows that we love him."

"I guess you're right," said Snow. "I'm going to be smart as well and go back to my fan."

Snow, Miss Pittypat, and Tonto parted ways, each one heading in a different direction.

By the third day there was still no sign of CougaMongaMingaMan. The group knew something was wrong. All three were worried and each had their own fears about what could have happened.

They were trying to decide what they should do, when the tall grass rustled. Miss Pittypat ordered, "Quiet!" and Tonto hissed. Suddenly, the grass parted and into their company walked a lovely Calico cat.

"Oh, thank goodness. It's Two-Face," said a relieved Snow. Miss Pittypat and Tonto uttered a greeting while inspecting her at the same time.

"Nice to meet you," Two-Face shyly replied. "I have news about CougaMongaMingaMan." All eyes fastened upon her as she continued.

"The other day I was hiding at the edge of the lot when CougaMongaMingaMan left your group. I had been keeping my eyes on a snake that had been hanging around. CougaMongaMingaMan didn't see me or the snake that was in his path." Two-Face paused briefly and then continued.

"I knew that he was in trouble so I jumped between them which startled both of them. Cougar jumped to the side but the snake was able to bite him on the tip of his tail because I heard him cry out."

Snow and Miss Pittypat started to shake and Tonto sat down. "What happened then?" they asked.

"We both ran home," Two-Face answered. "I think his humans have him inside because I haven't seen him and they look very worried."

"Let's go to his house and sit outside his window," suggested Miss Pittypat. Everyone agreed to the plan and off they went to CougaMongaMingaMan's house.

Tonto, Miss Pittypat, Snow, and Two-Face sat outside CougaMongaMingaMan's house and cried to him until his human opened the window and threw a bucket of water in their direction.

In the following week while waiting for news of their friend, the lot down the street underwent a transformation. The tall grass and weeds were removed and new sod was put down. Pathways were paved, trees were planted, picnic tables added, and a big fountain was installed in the middle.

Tonto, Miss Pittypat, Snow, and Two-Face observed the activities with interest.

"Isn't it nice the humans are building a park just for us?" sighed Miss Pittypat.

Snow was rubbing up against a tree when she looked up and saw CougaMongaMingaMan walking toward them with his tail proudly displayed straight up in the air. On the tip of his tail was a white bandage that he waved like a flag.

"Oh, hurrah!" they all called out. "You're back!" Everyone gathered around CougaMongaMingaMan to give him head nudges. "We were so worried."

Cougar looked at his companions and started purring. "I don't know what I would do without my friends, especially Two-Face."

Not used to being the center of attention, Two-Face began licking her paws. CougaMongaMingaMan said, "That snake bit me on the tail instead of my body because Two-Face jumped in to warn me. My tail is so long the poison was less harmful."

"Two-Face is a hero! We have our friend back and a new park to celebrate in!" declared Tonto.

As the group settled under the fountain to watch the nearby pigeons, CougaMongaMingaMan said to his friends, "This is the best day ever."

About the Author

Nancy was born and raised in Tampa, Florida, where her grandfather settled after arriving from England. She moved to Miami and then Lake Tahoe, Nevada, after attending college in Atlanta and London. She and her husband, Luigi, currently reside in Palos Verdes, California, along with CougaMongaMingaMan and his litter mate, Tilly, both of whom turned seventeen years old this year. Nancy happily traded in her nursing career to pursue her long-time interest in writing children's books. *CougaMongaMingaMan*, which will become a series based upon her cat, is the author's second published book. The author's first book, *Si, Mama, Si, Papa*, is a bi-lingual, Catholic/Christian children's book.

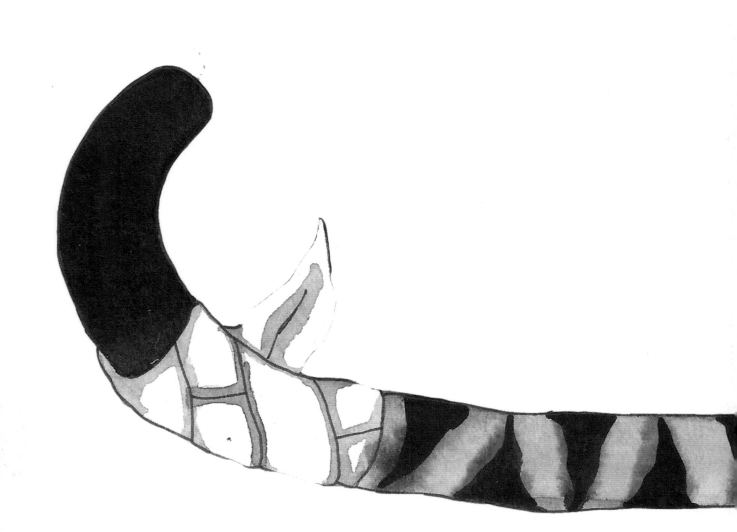